Joanne Green

PEACH

Joanne Green's stories have appeared in *The Philadelphia Inquirer*, *Writing Aloud*, and the anthology *Meridian Bound*. In addition to writing, she has worked as a costume and puppet designer for productions such as *The Muppet Show*, *Fraggle Rock*, and *The Great Muppet Caper*. She lives in Philadelphia with her husband and two children.

First published by GemmaMedia in 2012.
GemmaMedia
230 Commercial Street
Boston, MA 02109 USA

www.gemmamedia.com

Printed in the United States of America

16   15   14   13   12   1   2   3   4   5

978-1-934848-72-2

Library of Congress Cataloging-in-Publication Data

Green, Joanne, 1955–
  Peach / Joanne Green.
    p. cm.
  ISBN 978-1-934848-72-2
1.   Teenage girls—Fiction. 2.   Proms—Fiction.   I. Title.
  PS3607.R4329254P43 2012
  813'.6--dc23
          2012035968

Cover by Night & Day Design

Inspired by the Irish series of books designed for adult literacy, Gemma Open Door Foundation provides fresh stories, new ideas, and essential resources for young people and adults as they embrace the power of reading and the written word.

Brian Bouldrey
North American Series Editor

GEMMA
Open Door

For Tony

Track 1: Beautiful People

Melanie

I used to be ninety percent less cool. A rape thing happened and I sort of freaked out, but now I deal with it better than people who know. Or think they know—think that I put out for Jacob, some dude who tried to be nice to me, and know I had a miscarriage. At St. Ag's, girls stared in stone silence when I'd brave the bathroom to pee. First day back, somebody asked for my autograph! So for sophomore year, I started dragging my ass on the subway to Philadelphia Girls'. Now my friends are intellectuals. In South Philly, everybody talked about sex, liquor, and the Beatles. Here, they talk about sex, drugs, the Velvet

Underground, and Albert Camus. We yak in the bathroom about the Human Condition, which Albert Camus was supposed to be big on. Girls brag about their orgasms, and I keep my mouth shut.

Luna Dunkelman is my new best friend. She's far out. We sit on the school wall. This is illegal because perverts from all over Philly park their cars under there and beat off. They get hot if you squeal in horror. Instead, Luna yells, "Hey, pencil dick!" and laughs and laughs at the guy whamming away. They always leave.

Franco was walking by from the boys' school and thought she was talking to him. That's how we met.

Franco is so cool; his hair is almost as long as mine. And he has hair on his chest, really, but my little brother says it's just dirt. When people stare at Franco in his

2

Sergeant Pepper coat and John Lennon glasses, he doesn't hunch shorter like I do. Franco roars, "Take a picture—lasts longer!" and shoots them the finger.

That's what my father was like.

This year, I had to live down Woodstock. *Everybody* worth talking to in the whole tenth grade went to Woodstock. I want to hate my mom for not letting me go, but I didn't even know about it.

I hate her now. Now, everybody's going to Washington, D.C., for the big Moratorium. Everybody who's anybody is going to help stop the Vietnam War, and have a very cool time doing it!

Me, I'm going to the prom.

WORLD HISTORY
Peach Sweeney

Moratorium: mor · a · to · ri · um—
a formally agreed to period during
which activity is halted.

Kind of like a strike, except instead of
walking off from your job to get more
wages, we want the war to stop!

Track 2: We're Not Gonna Take It

The Who

If it was my prom, I could stay home. Or if it was at St. Ag's, I'd have a case to make. My mom's never even heard of the Moratorium. She thinks that some blockhead having a date to his prom is more important than our soldiers and our neighbors, and maybe someday Franco, dying in Vietnam.

I'm not even a date—I'm a cousin! James, Jamesie, is not exactly my cousin, he's my cousin Cookie's cousin. My cousin Cookie's loudmouth mother is related to me; my cousin Cookie's fat father is related to Jamesie. I haven't seen Jamesie in a while—since I freaked out, I don't go

5

to family gatherings. But Jamesie is seventeen, he's a senior, and he needs *me* for a date?

My mother says, "Don't jump to conclusions, Edith. You don't know what a fine young man he's become."

I know he's a blockhead.

He has to be. Me and Luna reasoned it out. We flipped through the family photos, and the thing is, Jamesie is *not bad looking*! He's shot up tall. Maybe his voice has finally changed, too. He's kind of cute, if he's your type—an Elvis pompadour with whitewalls around the ears, I swear. Nobody at Philadelphia Girls' would go out with him, but you think he'd be cute at Maple Tree Woods, which is in the stuffy suburbs.

And redundant, Luna says.

ENGLISH
Peach Sweeney

Redundant: re · dun · dant—with the same meaning as a word used earlier in a sentence.

The Department of Redundancy Department—ha!

Track 3: I Put a Spell on You

Creedence Clearwater Revival

The thing I can't even tell Luna is that Jamesie used to be my type. When I was in grade school, when I was fifty percent less cool, me and Jamesie used to fool around. We hid out in my cousin Cookie's bedroom, and while she sat, face all sneered up and huffy, me and Jamesie made out.

Jamesie, even if he is a probable blockhead, had this real genius for making out. I was too dazed to feel it then, but now when I'm in my room listening to "Light My Fire," sometimes I think of him, sliding his hand under my shirt, or slipping his tongue in my mouth.

I'd just die if anybody knew that.

After Cookie's mom and my mom and Jamesie's mother had the whole scene arranged, after I had a knock-out yell-fest with my mother, after I refused absolutely to go, after my mother told me to "be charitable," after she threatened to get the nuns over to talk to me, after she told me I was grounded forever if I didn't go: Jamesie called me.

My little brother runs by, stares at us standing there, and says, "Want me to get it?"

My mom snaps into action and grabs the phone.

Besides his Elvis haircut, did I say that Jamesie stutters? I hear this pathetic "Is-is-is E-e-e-e . . ." crackling through the line.

My mom doesn't even let him spit it out. She gushes, "Oh, Jamesie! Edith's right here!" I'm even more pissed off 'cause I told her a million times my name is Peach.

She hands me the phone and decides that now would be a really great time to dust the phone table and hum a lot.

I wait and let Jamesie ask me. It takes about five solid minutes for him to get it out. I pass the time by remembering all the tracks on the *Woodstock* album in order, from John Sebastian to Jimi Hendrix.

After his last hiss, I say, "But wouldn't you rather go to the Moratorium?"

He says, "Wh-wh-what?"

I roll my eyes. "The Moratorium," I explain. "It's this big antiwar protest. The government won't stop the war, so everybody's going to stop doing everything and go to D.C."

"So wh-wh-why do you have to go

to D-D-D.C.?" he asks. "You c-c-could s-s-stop doing everything at the p-p-p-p-prom, too!"

"But Allen Ginsberg's going to be there!" I protest. Though famous poets are probably not on Jamesie's must-see list.

I don't know what to say.

My mother mouths, "Be charitable." So I ask if there's going to be a band.

Oh, gross! The D-D-D-Duprees are going to play there—my *mom's* kind of music! I put my hand over the phone and hiss to my mom, "Maybe Jamesie should take *you*."

She swats me with the dust cloth, so I console him. "Well, Sha Na Na was at Woodstock."

Jamesie doesn't know who this jok-ey oldies band, Sha Na Na, is. Maybe he thinks I'm stuttering.

Nobody says anything.

I don't know where Jamesie's mom is, but she's nowhere near the phone. Jamesie says, "I th-th-think of you all the t-t-time, b-baby." He says he wants to kiss me all over in the d-d-d-dark.

I turn purple and say, "Look—I'll catch you at the prom."

I hang up. My mother's smiling and humming. Another smashing success for the Association of South Philadelphia Aunts. She needs to know what Jamesie said so she can report at the next meeting—in other words, as soon as she can get a dial tone.

I say, "Mom, he wants to *sodomize* me."

Her smile goes a little wonky, just for a second. Then she makes believe she didn't hear. I yell, "I just want you to know that I will never, ever live this down!"

She says, "Little one, it's a long life."

Everything my mother says would look good printed on a dish towel.

ANCIENT
~~WORLD~~ HISTORY
Peach Sweeney

The Prom Story, by Mrs. Sweeney (as told—1000 times—to Peach Sweeney)

"The Prom was the most wonderful night of my life. Your father was the best-looking boy in the room, with his broad shoulders and his lovely manners. We only danced a few dances, but I knew then that I wanted to spend the rest of my life with him. (Sobs.)"

The End

There's this picture of them that I've seen fifty times. They're on the dance floor at the gym, with paper roses for decorations in the background. When I was younger, I couldn't stop looking at it—not 'cause of the weird fancy clothes, the puzzling wrist corsage— but because my mom is smiling. She is actually happy.

Track 4: Somebody to Love

Jefferson Airplane

Franco doesn't say he wants to kiss me all
over in the d-d-dark on the phone. But
when we're in bed, he says, "Oh, baby,
baby, baby. I love you, I love you, I love
you."

Franco and me spend all our time in
bed. In South Philly, if you go all the way,
you're a slut. I asked Luna.

Luna says, "If somebody wants it, it's
a point of honor to share."

Franco definitely agreed.

I was sort of a virgin, in spite of the rape
stuff that happened. At least, I thought so,

and I wanted to hang on to the little bit that I had.

Me and Franco cut school and lay in bed at Luna's house. We'd get high and naked and crazy and do everything except go all the way—I mean, make love— I mean, you know what I mean. Franco talked a lot about love and sexual politics and brain damage.

Franco said, "Virginity is a form of brain damage."

HEALTH
Peach Sweeney

Sexual politics: sex · u · al pol · i · tics—having to do with the relationship between men and women, particularly in terms of power.

What? Huh?

Track 5: Ball and Chain

Janis Joplin

I go to mass with my mother and my brother. My brother ditches us right away to go sit with his buddies—he says, so he can make arm farts, but I know he's embarrassed. People still stare at me, Our Lady of the Miscarriage. I try to keep my eyes on the windows and the ceiling. In the chapel on the side aisle, there's a creepy statue of the Blessed Mother. I always feel like the BVM is eyeballing me, and that she doesn't like what she sees. When I look away, I glance back quick to see if her eyes have moved. My mom elbows me and tugs down her lace mantilla. Then I study the windows, two long rows of tall stained glass picturing the holy virgin martyrs. Like the saint they named my old school for, St. Agatha, who was some chick who got her tits lopped off for refusing to put out. It's like the Virginity Hall of Fame.

Father Nick usually beats this topic to death. Maybe because in confession all the St. Ag's girls tell him how they whisper the St. Aggie Story to their boyfriends when they're parked down the Lakes. Or is it paranoid to think Father nags because of *me*? When I told him about the rape thing Father Nick thought I made up a fairy tale.

"And who knows more about fairy tales than him?" Luna hooted.

I know she was just trying to make me feel better, but I thought lightning might strike her.

This time, Father Nick gives a sermon about Jacob and Esau, these two brothers. Esau, the older one, came back from hunting empty-handed and with a mean case of the munchies. The smell of the stew Jacob was cooking was so tempting and delicious that Esau forgot what was important. He sold his birthright to Jacob for a bowl of pottage from their kitchen stove. Then Father Nick turns his beady eyes on all the chicks in the church—or maybe just on me. He says, Giving up your cherished virginity is like that.

My mother lets out a sob and crosses herself.

I hang on to my still-attached tits and whisper, "Mom, there is no God."

That night, I let Franco do it.

WORLD HISTORY
Peach Sweeney

Bourgeois: bour · geois)—1. Of the middle class. 2. Overly concerned with being respectable and with material things. 3. In Marxist theory, of the social class that owns the means of producing wealth and is thought to take advantage of the working class.

Bouge—a shortened version of bourgeois, used by Luna to mean "just like everybody else," and not in a good way.

Track 6:
With a Little Help from My Friends

Joe Cocker

After weeks of sweating it that I was knocked up, Luna drags me to this old lez doctor who doesn't care if you're sixteen. Luna says she gives abortions in the basement, but we didn't see anything. I just pee in a jar.

Luna and I wait two hours in the tiny waiting room with cracked leatherette chairs. I picture the bright side of being pregnant—me and Franco could get married and be really cool parents and all.

Luna whoops, "Just like your mom." Then she flips, sneering, through *Good Housekeeping*.

When we finally go back in, I'm re-lieved, but a little sorry that I'm not pregnant.

The doctor, an old lady with nun shoes, sees that I'm kind of disappointed and lectures: "You must be responsible for your own sexuality, young woman."

You wouldn't think being called "young woman" could feel so bad.

Luna nods—she *so* sucks up to her. "You were so brave to get a medical de-gree, way back when," she coos. It's weird to hear Luna gush.

The doctor isn't any more impressed with Luna than with me. She hands me a blue prescription from a pad and waves us to the door.

I got the Pill. Then me and Franco never go anywhere for weeks. We used to go places, like museums on free days or the park, but now we just hang out in bedrooms. He can do it forever, which is really beautiful but pretty uncomfortable. One time I clocked it, he did it for two hours forty-five. In the girls' room, I made the mistake of telling Luna. She borrowed my wristwatch. And Frankie.

They both said, don't be so bouge.

HOME ECONOMICS
Peach Sweeney

Buffalo sandals: buf · fa · lo san · dals

Buffalo sandals are handmade in India from water buffalo hide. They have one decorated strap across your foot, and just one thong around your big toe.

To get them to fit, soak them in water while they are on your feet and let them dry. (While you do this, they smell like water buffalo—yuck!)

When you wear them, your feet are dirty all the time from dust and soot, and from wet stuff in the subway that you do not want to think about.

However, they are very cool.

Track 7: Purple Haze

Jimi Hendrix

Me and Luna buy some Indian bed-spreads. I make her a new dress to wear to the Moratorium. The dress is yellow. Franco hates yellow. Then I start my prom dress—black with pink and purple paisleys. I cut angel sleeves that have the border on them. I make it up as I go along, and it comes out a little crooked, but cool.

I'm going to do something really creative with my sewing someday. I tell Luna I want to make far-out clothes for deformed people to wear. Or else reflective orange vests for deer.

She says, "Snap out of it."

My mother eyes the prom dress. She says, "Very nice, dear," like it's a finger painting she's going to hang on the refrigerator.

Then she makes me go shopping with her. I want to go to California Earthquake or Purple Haze. We go to Sears.

I never go shopping with my mother. When she gets me past the door into the Junior Miss shop, she wiggles and smiles and makes little moans. I think she's going to orgazz right by the Bonnie Doone rack. She can't resist holding out a plaid kilt with a giant safety pin fastening the pleat—her dream. I rear back like Dracula from a silver crucifix. Then she pulls out dresses and holds them up to me. I hunch to about four feet tall and hang my hair in my eyes.

I drag her to the After Dark boutique and find this black strapless number with a slit skirt. I puff at my mother's red lipstick and make believe I'm smoking. I feel like a movie star.

My mother says, "Oh, Edith, you look so cheap."

I say, "Wake up, Mom. There's been a revolution."

She doesn't believe me.

We buy this white dress with *adorable* flowery trim and a stiff crinoline petticoat. I can picture Barbie, rifling through her closet before a big date with Ken, and when she sees this dress, cooing "Ooh, perfection!" It might look okay on Barbie. I feel like the Infant of Prague.

We hit the shoe department. The clerk gives the evil eye to my Indian water buffalo sandals and makes me put on those little nylon footies.

My mom apologizes to the guy for me not wearing stockings, and for the street dust on my feet. Then she tells him the whole Prom Story. "He's such a nice boy," she says about Jamesie.

I sink down in a vinyl chair near a foot mirror. "What about Franco?" I whisper.

She looks puzzled, then says to the clerk, "My Edith needs a nice boy." She adds, "Someone who will be able to overlook a lot."

"Know any guys with a seeing eye dog?" I ask the salesman, who ignores me. He knows who owns the Sears charge card in this family.

My mother—with the salesman on board—says I have to wear high heels. She says that everyone else will be wearing high heels.

I say that I will be wearing buffalo sandals.

She says, "Be outstanding by not standing out." She hands me a pair of gardenia-white kitten heels.

Then, I see them: the fuck-me pumps. I have this sudden jones for fuck-me pumps. These shoes have five-inch stiletto heels, a couple of toe things, and an ankle strap. And they're black!

My mom says, "It would look really cheap to wear black shoes with a white dress."

The clerk's with my mom till I say: "It would look really cheap to wear white shoes before Memorial Day." Got them there!

He stammers, and my mom says, "Proms are the exception to the 'No white shoes before Memorial Day' rule."

The clerk stares at my mom, and she blushes. Ladies don't fib.

We buy The Pumps in white.

MUSIC
Peach Sweeney

Jones: 1. drug withdrawal symptoms, especially from heroin; 2. an irresistible desire for something, like a heroin addict.

Like that Gil Scott-Heron and the Last Poets song, there's a " Jones Comin' Down."

Luna says that's the last song you'll hear before the Revolution comes.

Track 8: Volunteers

Jefferson Airplane

I wear my new black dress with pink and purple paisleys to the Moratorium send-off rally. I look far-out. Luna looks like a banana.

Me and Franco find a spot deep behind some bushes, and I let him do it. He does it for a really long time, while I look out for snoopers. I think, maybe if he does it enough, he won't do it with Luna in Washington, D.C.

I don't say this.

The college group has rented buses to take everybody to D.C. Franco and Luna get in line for the bus. I won't let go of Franco. This is very embarrassing for him. I hide behind my hair and cry. I don't make any noise.

Franco says, "Peach, you're too uptight. You can't love the world if you just love one person."

He holds me till the marshal guy closes the bus door.

Then I sit and smoke a joint with this guy who says he works at the Help Line. The Help Line is this phone number some rich drug dealer started, and you can call if you freak out. The guy has a deep, Help-Line kind of voice, but as he listens to my problem with Franco, he snakes his hand around me, wrinkling my bedspread dress.

He says, "You're a very beautiful person," and kisses me. When he presses his lips down hard, his tooth clicks against mine.

I cry harder. I want to love the whole world, but I just love Franco.

When I get home, I tell my mother, "I will never, ever forgive you."

Her eyes get watery. She reaches for me and says, "Weeping may tarry for a nightfall, but joy comes in the morning."

In the morning, I still hate her.

CHEMISTRY
Peach Sweeney

Marijuana: mar · i · jua · na—leaves of the plant *cannabis sativa*, used as an intoxicating drug. Also known as grass, weed, or boo.

Franco's an expert. He explains how weed is named for where it comes from. Like "Panama Red," "Thai Stick," or "Homegrown."

Joint—a cigarette containing marijuana. Also known as a doobie, a bomber (if large), or a roach (if the smoked-down end).

Franco's recipe for joints: Make sure no parents or little brothers are around.

Open an album cover and gently roll all sticks and seeds into the fold.

Crumple up the leaves and buds to a fine powder.

Use Zig-Zag cigarette rolling papers. Glue two papers together to make a longer sheet. Make a fold 1/3 from the bottom.

Gently sprinkle the weed into the crease.

Roll like a cigarette, only thinner.

Lick to seal. Light up and enjoy!

Track 9: I Feel Like I'm Fixin' to Die Rag

Country Joe McDonald and the Fish

I'm in my room, getting ready for the prom. I'm rolling fat bombers of Panama Red and stuffing them in my beaded clutch bag. I'm blasting Joe Cocker, "With a Little Help from My Friends." My little brother dusted off a Duprees album he found in the cellar, and is booming that. He thinks this is a laugh riot. Over this, I hear gasps of the assembled aunts and nuns downstairs, so I know that Jamesie has hit the scene. I put on The Dress.

My brother shoves his Batman glasses up his nose and stares at me. "You look like an asswipe," he shoots, then trots downstairs.

He tattled something. My mom creeps into my room, and she's smiling. This is always a bad sign.

My mother clears her throat and says, "Didn't you forget something, dear?" She whispers, "Edith, your foundation!"

We have a big fight about wearing a bra.

My brother smirks, "She doesn't have anything, anyway!"

I reach over my mom to clobber him and call him a pencil dick, but my mom's not listening, not even a little. She closes the door in his face.

She sits on the bed and explains her philosophy. She is the Jean-Paul Sartre of underwear.

I put on a bra.

Downstairs, in our parlor, are my cousin Cookie, Aunt Rita, Jamesie's mom, other aunts and three nuns. There are many uncles. Flashbulbs are popping in my face. I stagger with white flashes in my eyes and put on The Pumps. Nuns photograph me buckling them on. There's a sudden burst of ooh-ing. A hand takes my wrist and ties on a wrist corsage. This is Jamesie.

I keep my head tucked down. All I see is a ruffled pink shirt cuff and a pink tuxedo sleeve. The pink exactly matches the *adorable* pink flowery trim of my dress. I sense a conspiracy.

We stand in front of the mantelpiece and get photographed.

My mother shoves my hair back and says, "You have such a pretty face when you don't hide it," and then, "Smile."

I see my brother mouthing "asswipe."

Everybody walks us out to the white Thunderbird, Jamesie's dad's jalopy. It has bucket seats, fins, and a black vinyl roof, exactly the kind of greaser car that Sha Na Na would drive to make fun of themselves. Jamesie waxed it till the sunset gleams off it, except the black vinyl roof. Uncles whistle their appreciation of Jamesie's elbow grease. I can see he's worked hard, but I can't help noticing that it still looks like a four-wheeled saddle shoe.

My mom is holding my arm. I allow her to touch me only because I don't know how to walk in high heels. She's crying. This is how I know she's happy. "If only your father had lived to see this," she says.

I give her the meanest look I know, the one I usually save for my brother.

She whispers, "Bloom where you're planted, Edith."

I say, "There is no Edith!"

CHEMISTRY
Peach Sweeney

Sloe Gin: a red-colored sweet liqueur made from sloes (a plumlike fruit), gin, and sugar, with an alcohol content of about thirty percent.

Cough syrup with a kick!

Track 10: Coming into Los Angeles

Arlo Guthrie

Jamesie calls me P-P-Peach. When we drive off, he says, "Hey, P-P-Peach, here," and hands me a pint of sloe gin. "G-G-Girls like this."

I roll my eyes. I try to think of what Luna would say. Luna wouldn't be here. Maybe she would laugh at Jamesie, like she laughs at the perverts under the school wall. I picture Jamesie in the saddle-shoe car, speeding away like they do, all huffy.

"I'm not like any girls you know," I tell him.

He says, "Yeah!" and I know he's blushing. I blush, too. He reaches for my hand.

"Hey, how about a smoke?" I say, trying to keep it groovy. He slides a pack of Camels across the dash. I don't smoke cigarettes—that would be nasty. Instead, I pull out a bomber and light it.

This is what Jamesie says: "Shazam!"

He's really uptight. He push-button closes all the windows and peeks around for cops. He doesn't want any. I sit there and smoke by myself for a while.

Things start to get perfect. The car's all full of smoke, and the haze gives the sunset these really cool colors. I lean back in my bucket seat and put The Pumps on the black vinyl dash.

I decide I might be able to bring myself to look at Jamesie. This is what I see: a pink padded shoulder, mutton-chop sideburns, black curly hair just brushing his collar, a real cute smile. He still has buck teeth.

He looks at me. He says, "You l-look really p-p-pretty, Peach."

I decide to try to love him.

We cruise along without talking. The light is magic through the smoke. The radio plays that soft song, "Suite: Judy Blue Eyes," by Crosby, Stills, and Nash that they sang at Woodstock. Jamesie hums along. He doesn't stutter when he hums.

Father Nick would say that Jamesie is one of God's precious children. This is going to be all right.

HEALTH
Peach Sweeney

Cannabis intoxication:

can · na · bis in · tox · i · ca · tion—
the physical and mental results that
occur with cannabis use. Generally
described as a "high" feeling
followed by out-of-place joy or
laughter, and feelings of grandeur.
Other common signs include
reddening of the eyes, increased
appetite, dry mouth, and increased
heart rate. Negative effects include
inability to run large machinery,
paranoia, mood swings, depression,
and suicide.

To tell the truth, if my friends didn't smoke it, I might not bother.

But, you know, you can have the same negative effects anyhow, even if you don't smoke.

Track 11: Going Up the Country

Canned Heat

Then, we pull into the lot. The Log Cabin House Inn. I'm instantly mortified. It's gross. And redundant.

This guy, dressed like young Abe Lincoln in a flannel shirt and sawed-off pants with only one suspender, is helping girls out of cars. I laugh, but one look from Jamesie, and I try to mask it as a sputter. A sputter that sounds like a stutter. A sputter-stutter, complete with spit-lets.

Jamesie shrugs and say, "Is that guy b-b-begging for a wedgie, or wh-what?"

I break up. Laugh and spit and sputter rain all over the car, then I try to snap out of it. Wedgie jokes? This is the kind of immature stuff I used to laugh at when I hung out with Jamesie. Albert Camus wouldn't laugh at an exploited worker with underwear caught in his ass crack, I know it.

I say, "I feel really sorry for Abe."

Jamesie smiles and brushes my hair away from my eyes. I blush.

We park in the far end of the lot. I light a match to finish the bomber. I need just a little more help before I can go inside.

Jamesie smokes, too. He takes little puffs and blows them out right away. Then he yells, "Shit, fuck, damn!"

This is what we used to do when the grown-ups would leave us in the house alone. Cousin Jamesie, Cousin Cookie, and me would watch to see the grown-ups pull away, Jamesie's mom and dad in the

saddle-shoe car. We'd wait till they turned
the corner. Then we'd crank the stereo to
the max and yell curses over and over.

He makes me yell it with him. We sit
in the car, smoking and yelling, "Shit,
fuck, damn!"

I laugh till the tears leak, but I wish I
didn't think it was funny.

I really can't walk in The Pumps now.
Jamesie comes around and opens the car
door. My feet wobble like Minnie Mouse's.
He holds me. He holds me closer. Any
closer, and I might get a wedgie. Instead, I
get the shakes. Jamesie offers to give me his
jacket. This is very bouge behavior. Franco
would never act like this. Franco knows
I am a person, equal to himself, and that
I am responsible for my own body tem-
perature. Still, I'm shivering.

Jamesie whispers, "You l-look really s-s-swell, Peach."

I say, "I have a boyfriend."

Then I say, "Thanks."

~~ALGEBRA~~ PHILOSOPHY

Peach Sweeney

If $A^2 + B^2 = C^2$, and B = 12, how many solutions are there in which C is a prime number?

How can you love the whole world?

Is this what Jesus had in mind?

Is it better to let yourself be raped, or to cut off your tits and die, like St. Agnes?

Wouldn't you help more people if you didn't die?

You could teach them about love, right?

Is it okay if you live and you try really hard to be a good person?

Track 12: At The Hop

Sha Na Na

Jamesie holds open the log door of the Cabin House. Inside are no nuns, but lots and lots of flashbulbs. Through the white spots the flashes make in my eyes, I see Jamesie's friends. All the guys look like Easter eggs. All the chicks look like toaster dolls. I outstandingly don't stand out. I look for the powder room to ditch the bra.

The bathrooms are labeled "Abes" and "Babes." In "Babes," girls are ratting their hair. They are gobbing on makeup. Of course, I'm not wearing makeup. They feel sorry for me and offer me some. I don't know what to say. If I decorate myself with cosmetics, I'll be a tool of the beauty industry.

I say, "No, thanks. I don't want to look cheap." They believe me.

At the log picnic tables with fancy white tablecloths, we eat fruit cup. The log seat snags on my stockings.

Jamesie's best friend, in a lavender tux, is a real whoopee cushion. He tells dead baby jokes. "What do you call a dead baby with no arms and legs on your doorstep?"

"Matt!!!" he hoots.

His date, in a lavender tent dress, giggles at his jokes and chats with me. She whispers, "Jamesie's a real catch!" She waves her hand as if to cool herself off.

I make my eyes wide and ask, "A catch like in softball? A catch like pneumonia?"

She says, "You know, a catch! Like you catch him and get hitched—married!"

She tries really hard to explain to me all of Jamesie's good points: tall, hunky, nice. When I ask for more details, she frowns, puzzled, and says, "He's nice."

"Besides," she explains, "this is the most important night of the year! Of your whole life!"

"You mean, this is your peak?" I ask her, my jaw hanging open. "It's all downhill from *here*?"

"Oh, right!" she backtracks. "Except your wedding day. Second-most important!"

Jamesie's friend has another one for us: "What's black and white and red and won't fit through a revolving door?"

"A nun with a spear through her head!" He slaps his knee and guffaws.

Jamesie's pals all roar like hyenas.

"You should be on T-T-T-TV," Jamesie says, in awe.

Jamesie's friend's date says in a sing-song-y voice, "So, tell all! How'd you two meet?"

Suddenly, Jamesie is all ears. Before I can answer, he grips my hand. "Peach, do you know any j-j-jokes?"

I think hard, then say, "What has big jowls and bombs millions of innocent Cambodians?"

Nobody knows the answer. If they did know, they might be at the Moratorium right now, protesting President Nixon and the Vietnam War.

Instead, Jamesie's friend rolls his eyes and asks, "What do you call a dead baby with no arms and legs that floats in your pool?"

"Bob!!!"
They split their sides laughing.

WORLD HISTORY
Peach Sweeney

Cambodia: Cam · bo · di · a—
a country in Southeast Asia,
bordering Vietnam, that remains
neutral in the U.S.-Vietnam
conflict.

The U.S. is supposed to be holding peace
talks, but instead, our air force has
been secretly bombing Cambodia. Even
if there are supply bases there for the
bad guys, we still shouldn't be bombing
some little country!

Track 13: Joe Hill

Joan Baez

I go outside to get more psychedelic. Before I can light up, this guys pulls up on a motorcycle. He's wearing a *black* tux. He must be lost, I think. He eyeballs me in my prom gown, does a double take, then flags me down. He says, "Hey, tits—want to straddle my machine and get a buzz on?"

I do!

But I don't. He lets Abe park his bike and hands me a skinny joint. "Thai Stick. Bad ass," he says. It is.

I see my reflection in his sunglasses. At first, I rear back. I don't know it's me—the long-haired chick in the First Communion frock. Then I just wished it wasn't.

I say, "My boyfriend's in D.C. at the Moratorium."

He says, "Cool."

He looks me over again. "And what brings you here, babe?"

I don't know what to say. After a long time, I explain, "I'm exploring the Human Condition."

Motorcycle Guy doesn't say anything to that one. He just looks at me. Even with dark glasses on, I know exactly the way he's looking at me. He's gazing at me exactly the way that Jacob's brother, Esau, stared at that bowl of pottage.

"Hey, want some mints?" I say in a teeny voice. I'm dry, cotton-mouthed. I reach in my clutch bag and fish out some

Sen-Sen. While I shake open the packet, he grabs the bra from my bag. He puts it on his head. It makes little bunny ears on top of his blond head.

I say, "My mother would like you."

He doesn't believe me.

He takes the bra off. He puts the mints away. He sniffs my wrist corsage, then kisses my hand. Not the back of my hand, like some French guy, like maybe Jean-Paul Sartre himself might try. He kisses the palm. He holds the palm over his full lips and kisses it with his tongue.

It's like something Franco would do, if he wasn't getting down to business, which he always is. If he wasn't, he'd do this, I know it.

I feel a shadow over me. I think it's a symbol, like in a poem, but then I notice that the shadow blocks the light that reflects in Motorcycle Guy's sunglasses.

Jamesie has found me.

The dude lowers my hand, but he doesn't let go of it. He's holding my hand, and I feel it right down to The Pumps. I feel a breeze, and I shiver. "It's way too cold for motorcycles," I say. I take a wobbly step. The guy is still holding my hand as the three of us go inside.

FRENCH
Peach Sweeney

Souvenirs de Mon Père

Mon père m'a appris à danser. Il m'a porté sur ses pieds et m'a appris à mettre ma main gauche sur son épaule, et de tenir sa droite. Il a mis un disque à l'ancienne, et compta les battements. Même si je vacille sur ses gros souliers, je me sentais en sécurité. Je me sentais en sécurité comme je n'ai jamais ressenti depuis. Je me souviens.

My father taught me to dance. He stood me on his feet and taught me to put my left hand on his shoulder,

and to hold his right. He put an old-
fashioned record on the record player
and counted out the beat. Even though
I teetered on his heavy shoes, I felt
safe. I felt okay in a way that I don't
feel anymore. I remember.

Track 14: Dance to the Music

Sly & the Family Stone

Inside, the Duprees are playing their greatest, "You Belong to Me." It's the big moment. Jamesie wants to dance.

Dance? I don't dance. I especially can't dance with the cool guy watching. "Nobody dances," I say.

"B-but everybody is d-dancing," Jamesie says. His wave shows all the dancing pairs of Crayola colors, eyes shut, grooving to the D-Duprees. He puts his arms around me.

The motorcycle guy's hand slips from mine. I watch his grin as Jamesie moves me across the floor.

I keep falling off my heels, but Jamesie

doesn't care. He holds me. He doesn't care if nobody dances, or if I look like an ass-wipe, or if I don't remember to follow. He holds me really close. He grinds against me. I get the shakes.

Jamesie pushes my hair away from my face and kisses me, really slow and beautiful. In my ear, he breathes, "S-s-see the pyramids along the N-N-Nile. . . ."

The log tables behind us are empty. Everybody is crowding the dance floor. They clutch each other, swaying their bodies to the same rhythm. The colors swirl around us. Jamesie's friend is holding his date close. As they pass, she gives out a little gasp of pleasure. I think of the Maple Tree Woods-ers as colorful birds, and their getups don't seem so silly. As Jamesie says, it's the big moment. Maybe the biggest moment in their lives. Not everybody has been raped, or had a parent die, or had Father Nick's beady eyes staring at them. For some people, the biggest moment is something happy, like this.

I close my eyes. I remember how to dance. I remember what it's like to be held and to feel okay. I forget who I am. I feel good.

HEALTH
Peach Sweeney

Trojan: Tro · jan—1. A citizen of ancient Troy; 2. Someone who is strong and brave; 3. A popular brand of prophylactics, used for contraception.

"Sealed in foil for your protection."

Track 15: I Want to Take You Higher

Sly & the Family Stone

Then we're in Jamesie's car.

He holds the door and helps me in. His good manners don't seem nearly as bouge now. I could get used to it. Jamesie gives me a big grin, and I smile. Without trying too hard, even.

We ride along in the T-Bird, listening to the radio: "Everything is beautiful in its own way." Instead of the song sounding sappy like it always does, I get teary. Maybe the prom *is* as beautiful as standing up for what you believe in at the Moratorium. Not to me, for sure, but to Jamesie's friend, and maybe even to him. Maybe they're God's precious children, too, almost as much as those poor Cambodians are.

I get in a Maple Tree Woods groove.

I think we're at a really long red light. Then I notice that Jamesie has cut the engine. The saddle-shoe car is parked in the old Stetson factory parking lot. The lot is huge and midnight dark. It looks like nobody's been here for a couple of years.

"Why don't people wear hats anymore?" I ask Jamesie. The streetlights from way behind us reflect off the dark factory windows, and I see that some of them are broken. "People should wear hats so other people can get jobs making them."

Jamesie downs a big sip from the Sloe Gin pint. He says, "G-g-give me my g-g-goodbye now!"

He clamps his lips on my mouth. Then his tongue presses in there. He kisses me for a really long time. His hands (are there just two of them?) slip under the pink flowery trim of my prom dress. I squeeze between the seat and the door till I can't make myself any smaller. I feel myself starting to leave my body.

All out of breath, Jamesie snorts, "It's not like you're a v-v-virgin."

Ouch!

But he is, I remember. I start crying. At first, I don't know why I'm crying, but then I think, it's way, way too sad. Making love is such a beautiful thing. It's supposed to be beautiful. Jamesie doesn't know how beautiful it is. I touch his hair. I let him kiss me some more, even though his spit kind of drips down my dress.

I whisper, "I wish we weren't in a car. I want everything to be really beautiful for you."

He tears off his clip-on bow tie and loosens his ruffled shirt. He levers the bucket seat back and presses on top of me. I keep moving my fancy heels on the floor, so I remember it's there. "I have feet—this time, I can leave if I want," I tell myself, like a mantra.

His hands are under my dress, but I keep sneaking it back down. I can't quite see his face in the dark, but mostly, it's kind of like he's not in there. I know that look—I wish I didn't.

Then I hear a zipper and the crinkle of tinfoil, and about three seconds later—ouch!—it's over.

I'm glad he used a Trojan, 'cause I don't want to chance even a little getting his baby in me. Jamesie wouldn't be a cool parent. I don't love him like I love Franco.

But I do love him? I have to love him,

right? I love Jamesie the way I love everybody else in the whole world.

It's hot in the car, and I can't help noticing that his sweat is getting a little smelly. I also notice that when Jamesie moans, he doesn't stutter either. And he does moan. He uses up the whole three-pack. I can't stop crying.

After he finishes, Jamesie says, "Yahoo!"

I don't feel like cheering.

ENGLISH
Peach Sweeney

Miscarriage: mis · car · riage
1. the forcing out of a fetus before it is able to live outside the body, especially between the third and seventh months of pregnancy;
2. failure to achieve the right, or desired result: a miscarriage of justice; 3. failure of something sent, as a letter, to reach its destination.

Track 16: I'm Going Home

Ten Years After

Jamesie gets out of the car. I hear splashing on the asphalt as he takes a whiz. I wriggle my pantyhose back up. I feel sticky and sore—and something else, something I don't want to think about. When Jamesie comes back, he is all buttoned and zipped. He looks different. He is different. Now he knows what life's all about, or he thinks he does.

Then we are driving. Jamesie keeps glancing over at me, grinning. I see him out of my side vision, because I am looking out the window. I try to remember how far it is to home.

Jamesie smiles at me. He says, 'I kn-kn-knew I'd get l-l-l-l-lucky!"

I tell him that this was a very serious thing.

He absolutely agrees. He wants another date so we can do this serious thing some more.

I say, except it comes out as a squeak, "Maybe," but he can tell I don't mean it.

"And why not?" he demands.

Some riddles aren't supposed to have answers.

He won't let it go. I remind him— I told him to begin with—that I have a boyfriend.

"Wh-wh-what's he got that I haven't got?" he wants to know.

Me. That's what Franco has. I'm not much, but I'm his. I mean, if it is okay to belong to just one person.

I say, "Jamesie, you're a beautiful human being."

He says, "You're a s-s-slut!" He means it.

I laugh, like Luna would laugh, when she gasps and says, "I'm a slut! I'm a slut!"

I laugh, but I don't think it's funny.

HOME ECONOMICS
Peach Sweeney

Home: 1. Residence—the place where a person or family lives; 2. Birth place—the place where somebody was born or raised or feels that he belongs; 3. Safe place—a place where a person or animal can find refuge or safety or live in security.

"Most of you girls will grow up to be housewives."

Luna raises her hand and asks, "Will that be on the test, Mrs. Kornberg?"

Track 17: Soul Sacrifice

Santana

Jamesie takes me home. He doesn't get out and open the door, not now. That's okay—it's just some bouge custom, I remind myself, as I wobble up the walk to my front door.

There are no nuns taking pictures now. No neighbors, no uncles. Just my mother. She has a dreamy look in her eyes. She wants to know all about it.

When I don't say anything, my mother begins to recite "The Prom Story." Though I've sat through it a hundred times, I can't listen to it even once more.

I roar, "Mom, he fucked me three times."

"Whoa!" my little brother hoots.

My mother tries to make believe she doesn't hear it. Her face frowns, concentrating, like she's telling herself, "I don't hear it, I don't hear it, I don't hear it." But this time she just can't pull that off.

All teary, she kisses me and says, "You're one of God's precious children, Edith."

I suddenly hate her more than I have ever hated anybody. I get her hand in a death grip till her curlers rattle, and I say, "There . . . is . . . no . . . Edith!"

Her smile gets really wonky this time.

This time, *she* stutters, "W-W-W . . . Y-Y-You . . . Oh, my!"

I'm not sure, but I think she finally believes me.

When I tell Franco, he's not as cool as you'd think. He flips out.

I try to explain, "I just tried to love Jamesie the way I love the whole world."

"And are you going to give the whole world a mercy fuck?" Franco hollers. Something you'd never hear Albert Camus say.

"Uncool," Luna butts in.

I cry. Sometimes, in between doing it to me, Franco argues some more. Then he says, "Oh, baby, baby, baby."

It's really beautiful.

PEACH: A Reader's Guide

About the Book

Peach Sweeney is a sixteen-year-old girl caught in confusing times. Against the backdrop of the tumultuous 1960s, with the sexual revolution, the Vietnam War protests, and the Women's Liberation Movement all in full swing, Peach struggles with her own heartache—a rape in her past, a dead parent, and friends with new and strange ideas. Then family pressure forces this flower child in sandals to attend a cousin's high school prom. There, her new ideas clash with neighborhood tradition as she searches for an answer to the question: How can you love the whole world if you just love one person?

About the Author

Joanne Green grew up in working-class Philadelphia, *American Bandstand* territory, in a tight-knit extended family. Like Peach, Joanne came of age at a time of quickly changing social customs, a time when guys who hung out on street corners singing doo-wop suddenly traded in their leather jackets for bell-bottom jeans and electric rock music. Also like Peach, Joanne left her conservative South Philly neighborhood to attend a magnet public high school fifteen miles north—and a world away—from home. Going to school with girls from wealthier, more educated families gave her the sense that she was an outsider, and not at home in either world.

Joanne grew up listening to storytellers, whether at family gatherings or while eavesdropping outside the neighborhood taproom. She believes that we all have a storyteller within us and that, like Peach, we don't need a huge vocabulary to tell a story—especially if we are willing to make up a few words.

Before you read:

- Look at the picture on the cover. What does the picture make you think the story will be about?
- Most books are divided into chapters. *Peach* is divided into "tracks," each named for a song on the main character's favorite album. How does this fit with a teenaged narrator? Do you have a favorite song that fits with a major event in your life?
- *Peach* is partly about what it feels like to be in a strange new environment where people have unfamiliar ideas. Can you think of a time when you left home or began at a new school or job?

What were some of the puzzling new things you noticed? How did you feel about yourself in this new place?

As you read:

Look for answers to these basic questions:

- **Who** tells the story?
- **What** happens to Peach in the story?
- **Where** does most of the story take place?
- **When** is the story set?
- **Why** does Peach go to the prom?
- **How** does Peach feel about Jamesie? About Franco?
- **How** does Peach change her ideas about both boys—and about herself?

After you read:

Focus: Titles

- Is "Peach" a good title for this book? What are the different meanings of the word *peach*? How do they relate to the book?
- Author Joanne Green's original title for the story was *There's Been a Revolution*. Why do you think she chose that title? What makes a good title for a book?

- Each chapter is named for a song on *Woodstock*, Peach's favorite album. How do the titles, or "tracks," relate to each chapter?
- Some chapter titles in *Peach* relate to the action of the story and others relate to the mood of each chapter. Choose a title and tell how it adds to or takes away from the story.

Focus: Characters

- As the book's narrator, Peach gives little physical description of the major characters. How did you picture these characters? Describe them using words and sentences from the book and add some ideas of your own.
- How accurate is Peach's description of her mother? What else can you imagine about the mother's life besides what Peach says? Do you feel sympathy for the mother? Why or why not?
- What kind of person is Franco? Describe his character. How well does he know Peach? Does Franco have Peach's best interests at heart? Repeat these questions with the other characters.
- What do the characters' names—including Jamesie's—tell you about them? Why does

Peach make up a new name for herself? Is "Luna" her friend's real name? Do you have more than one name—one you use in your family and a different name your friends or co-workers use?

- Peach's father is mentioned, but he never appears in the book. Is he still an important character in the story? Why or why not?

Focus: Setting
- *Peach* is set in three very different places in Philadelphia: Peach's home in South Philadelphia; Peach's new high school, which is a long subway ride away; and Maple Tree Woods, the suburban area where Jamesie lives. How are these settings different? What are the different rules and values Peach describes for each of these settings? What problems do these differences cause for Peach?
- In what ways have you felt like Peach when you traveled to a different location, whether across town or across the globe?
- *Peach* is set in 1970, just after the rock festival Woodstock, which took place in 1969. What do you know about Woodstock? Do a Google image search and look at pictures from this

festival. How do these images compare with
what you imagined while reading the book?

- What political events does Peach refer to? In
  what ways does the outside world seem to be
  changing in the story?

- How sincere is Peach's commitment to the
  Vietnam War protests?

- In what ways does the historical setting for
  Peach shape the story's characters and deter-
  mine what happens? What would be different in the story if it took place today?

Focus: Point of View

- Everything we know in the story is told to us
  by Peach, the narrator. What details does she
  give? What information does she leave out?
  How accurate is what Peach says?

- Imagine telling this story to a friend. How
  would the story be different from how Peach
  tells it? What would you add to the story?
  What would be lost?

- Imagine that another character is the narrator of the story. Tell the story from Jamesie's
  point of view—or a different character's. Is
  it a different story? Is it a story you would
  prefer to read?

Focus: Action
- Why does Peach go to the prom with Jamesie?
- Have you ever been to a prom or formal dance? Were you excited to go, or did you go for another reason? Do you think a prom is "the second-biggest evening of your life," as one of Jamesie's friends says?
- Why does Peach submit to Jamesie? In what ways does her experience of rape (before the story begins) affect her actions? Have you ever been in a situation in which you felt uncomfortable with what was happening, but didn't feel able to stop it?

Focus: Language
- Peach chooses some unusual words, some of which she makes up, for example, *bouge* or *orgazz*. Why does she use these words? Did you always understand what she was trying to say? What do these words add to or take away from the story?
- Do you, your friends, or your family have words that have unique meanings within your group? Give some examples of any of these words. Why do you use them? If you speak another language, are there some

words that don't translate to English? Give examples.

- How do the pages from Peach's notebook add to the story? Do the definitions give helpful information? In what ways does Peach show a different side of herself in her notebook?
- How does Peach's word choice add to the humor of the story?
- Peach is concerned about the meanings of words. Think of some words from the story that are used in different ways (for example, the words *slut* or *miscarriage*). What are the different meanings? How do these words add meaning to the story?

Focus: Humor

- Some readers describe this as a sad story, others as a funny story. What do you think?
- Imagine the story without humor. What is left of the story? Is it a story you would prefer reading?
- Give an example of a sentence from the story you find especially funny. What is Peach really saying in this sentence? Is Peach's humor mean-spirited? In what ways, if any, does she laugh at herself?

Focus: Ending

- When Peach tells Franco about her experience with Jamesie, she says, "He's not as cool as you'd think." Are you surprised at Franco's reaction? How does his reaction fit with his ideas as he had told them to Peach?
- Is Peach the same person at the end of the story as she was at the beginning? What, if anything, has she learned?
- Imagine Peach five years after the end of the story. What will she be doing? Will she still be friends with Luna? Will she still be with Franco?
- Do you think that Peach's life will have a happy ending? Why or why not?